THE ALIENIST

Machado de Assis

2024

THE ALIENIST

BY

MACHADO DE ASSIS

TRANSLATED

BY

RODOLFO MEDEIROS

EDITION
2024

BY

SOFIA PUBLISHER

Copyright © Sofia Publisher, 2024

Title:

THE ALIENIST

Author:

Machado de Assis

Translator:

Rodolfo Medeiros

Edited and illustrated by:

Sofia Publisher, 2024

Table of Contents

Chapter I: How Itaguai Gained a House of Madmen 9

Chapter II: Torrents of Madmen.................17

Chapter III: God Knows What He Does.................25

Chapter IV: A New Theory 31

Chapter V: The Terror 37

Chapter VI: The Rebellion 55

Chapter VII: The Unexpected.................65

Chapter VIII: The Apothecary's Agonies 71

Chapter IX: Two Beautiful Cases.................75

Chapter X: Restoration 79

Chapter XI: The Astonishment of Itaguai 87

Chapter XII: The End of Paragraph 4.................91

Chapter XIII: Plus Ultra! 101

Chapter I: How Itaguai Gained a House of Madmen

Itaguai

The chronicles of the village of Itaguai say that in ancient times, a certain doctor lived there, Dr. Simon Bacamarte, the son of the local nobility and the greatest physician in Brazil, Portugal, and Spain. He had studied in Coimbra and Padua. At the age of thirty-four, he returned to Brazil, as the king could not persuade him to stay in Coimbra, leading the university, or in Lisbon, handling the affairs of the monarchy.

— The science, — he told His Majesty, — is my sole occupation; Itaguai is my universe.

Having said that, he immersed himself in Itaguai, dedicating himself wholeheartedly to the study of science, alternating between healing and reading, and demonstrating theorems with poultices. At the age of forty, he married Mrs. Evarista da Costa e Mascarenhas, a lady of twenty-five, a widow of a judge from outside, not beautiful or amiable. One of his uncles, a paca[1] hunter before the Eternal, and no less frank, was astonished at such a choice and expressed it to him. Simon Bacamarte explained that Mrs. Evarista possessed physiological and anatomical conditions of the first order; she digested easily, slept regularly, had a good pulse, and excellent vision. Thus, she was suitable for bearing him robust, healthy, and intelligent children. If, in addition to these qualities, — the only ones worthy of a wise man's concern, — Mrs. Evarista was poorly composed in features, far from lamenting it, he thanked God for it, as he would not run the risk of neglecting the interests of science in the exclusive, petty, and vulgar contemplation of his consort.

Mrs. Evarista disappointed Dr. Bacamarte's hopes, giving him neither robust nor feeble children. The natural temperament of science is patience; our doctor waited three years, then four, then five. After that time, he made a profound study of the matter, reread all the Arab and other writers he had brought to Itaguai, sent inquiries to Italian and German universities, and ended up advising his wife on a special diet. The illustrious lady, nourished exclusively with the good pork of Itaguai, did not heed her husband's admonitions. And due to her resistance, — explainable but inexcusable, — we owe the complete extinction of the Bacamarte dynasty.

But science has the ineffable gift of healing all sorrows;

· · · · · · ·

[1] [Paca is the second largest rodent in Brazil in terms of size, behind only capybaras.]

our doctor immersed himself entirely in the study and practice of medicine. It was then that one of its corners particularly caught his attention, — the psychic corner, the examination of cerebral pathology. In the colony and even in the kingdom, there was not a single authority in such a matter, poorly explored or almost unexplored. Simon Bacamarte understood that Lusitanian science, and particularly Brazilian science, could be adorned with "evergreen laurels", — an expression he himself used, but in a moment of domestic intimacy; externally, he was modest, as befits the knowledgeable.

— The health of the soul, — he exclaimed, — is the most worthy occupation of the physician.

— Of the true physician. — added Crispin Soares, the town apothecary, one of his friends and tablemates.

The town council of Itaguai, among other sins accused by chroniclers, had the sin of not taking care of the mentally ill. Thus, every furious madman was locked in a chamber, in his own house, not cured but uncured until death came to deprive him of the benefit of life; the tame ones roamed freely in the streets. Simon Bacamarte immediately understood the need to reform such a bad custom. He requested permission from the council to house and treat in the building he was going to construct all the madmen of Itaguai, and of other towns and cities, with a stipend that the council would provide when the family of the patient could not. The proposal aroused the curiosity of the entire town and met with great resistance, as it is true that absurd or even bad habits are not easily up-rooted. The idea of putting the madmen in the same house, living together, seemed in itself a symptom of madness, and there was no shortage of those who insinuated it to the doctor's own wife.

Father Lopes

— Look, Mrs. Evarista, — said Father Lopes, the local vicar, — see if your husband takes a trip to Rio de Janeiro. This business of studying all the time is not good; it turns the mind.

Mrs. Evarista was horrified; she went to her husband and told him that "she had cravings," especially the desire to come to Rio de Janeiro and eat everything that seemed suitable for a certain purpose to him. But that great man, with the rare sagacity that distinguished him, understood his wife's intention and replied with a smile, telling her not to be afraid. He then went to the council, where the councilors were debating the proposal, and defended it with such eloquence that the majority decided to authorize what he had requested, simultaneously voting for a tax to subsidize the treatment, lodging, and maintenance of poor lunatics. Finding a suitable subject for the tax was not easy; everything in Itaguai was already taxed. After long studies, it was decided to allow the use of two plumes on the horses of funerals. Anyone who wanted to plume the horses of a funeral carriage would pay two pennies to the council, with this amount repeating as many times as the hours between the time of death and the last blessing at the burial. The clerk got lost in the arithmetic calculations of the potential revenue from the new tax, and one of the councilors, who did not believe in the doctor's project, asked to exempt the clerk from useless work.

— The calculations are not precise, — he said, — because Dr. Bacamarte doesn't accomplish anything. Who has seen all the lunatics now being put in the same house?

The worthy magistrate was mistaken; the doctor arranged everything. Once granted the license, he immediately began to build the house. It was at the New Street, the most beautiful street in Itaguai at that time; it had fifty windows on each side, a courtyard in the center, and numerous cubicles for the guests. As he was a great Arabist, he found in the Quran that Mohammed declares the insane venerable, considering that Allah takes away their reason so that they do not sin. The idea seemed beautiful and profound to him, and he had it engraved on the facade of the house. However, fearing the vicar, and indirectly the bishop, he attributed the thought to Benedict VIII, deserving, with this fraud, albeit pious, that Father Lopes told him the life of that eminent pontiff at lunch.

The Green House

The asylum was named Green House, alluding to the color of the windows, which appeared green for the first time in Itaguai. It was inaugurated with immense pomp; people from all nearby and even distant towns and villages, and from the city of Rio de Janeiro itself, came to witness the ceremonies that lasted for seven days. Many lunatics were already admitted, and relatives had the opportunity to see the paternal care and Christian charity with which they would be treated. Mrs. Evarista, extremely pleased with her husband's glory, dressed luxuriously, adorned herself with jewels, flowers, and silks. She was a true queen on those memorable days; everyone visited her two or three times, despite the modest and reserved customs of the time, and not only courted her but also praised her. This fact is a highly honorable testament to the society of the time because they saw in her the happy wife of a lofty spirit, of an illustrious man, and if they envied her, it was the holy and noble envy of admirers.

After seven days, the public festivities came to an end; Itaguai finally had a nuthouse.

Chapter II: Torrents of Madmen

Three days later, in an intimate conversation with the apothecary Crispin Soares, the alienist unveiled the mystery of his heart.

Simon Bacamarte and Crispin Soares

— Charity, Mr. Soares, certainly plays a part in my conduct, but it enters as a seasoning, like the salt of things. That's how I interpret what Saint Paul said to the Corinthians: "If I understand all the mysteries and all knowledge, and have not charity, I am nothing." The main focus of my work at Green House is to study madness deeply, its various degrees, classify its cases, ultimately discover the cause of the phenomenon, and the universal remedy. This is the mystery of my heart. I believe that in doing this, I render a good service to humanity.

— An excellent service. — corrected the apothecary.

— Without this asylum, — continued the alienist, — I could do little. However, it provides me with a much greater field for my studies.

— Much greater. — added the other.

And he was right. From all the neighboring towns and settlements, madmen flocked to Green House. There were furious ones, docile ones, monomaniacs, the entire family of the spirit's outcasts. After four months, Green House was a small town. The initial cubicles were not enough; an annex of another thirty-seven was added. Father Lopes confessed that he had never imagined the existence of so many madmen in the world, let alone the inexplicable nature of some cases. For example, there was a coarse and villainous young man who, every day after lunch, delivered a scholarly discourse adorned with tropes, antitheses, apostrophes, with its Greek and Latin embellishments, and its tassels from Cicero, Apuleius, and Tertullian. The vicar could hardly believe it. What! A young man he had seen playing shuttlecock in the street just three months before!

— I'm not saying it's not true, — the alienist replied, — but the truth is what Your Reverence is seeing. This happens every day.

— As for me, — the vicar added, — it can only be explained by the confusion of languages at the Tower of Babel, as Scripture tells us. Probably, since languages were confused in ancient times, it's easy to exchange them now, as long as reason doesn't work…

— That may indeed be the divine explanation of the phenomenon, — the alienist agreed after a moment of reflection, — but it's not impossible that there is also some human, purely scientific reason, and that's what I am investigating.

— Alright, be that as it may, and I am anxious. Truly!

The ones that got mad by love were three or four, but only two stood out for the curious nature of their delusions. The first, a young man named Falcon, aged twenty-five, believed himself to be the morning star. He would stretch out his arms and legs to give them a certain appearance of rays, and would spend hours asking if the sun had already risen for him to retire. The other one was constantly, endlessly, always walking around the rooms or the courtyard, along the corridors, searching for the end of the world. He was a wretch whose wife left him for following a whim. As soon as he discovered her escape, he armed himself with a blunderbuss and pursued them. Two hours later, he found them near a pond, and killed them both with the utmost cruelty.

Jealousy was satisfied, but the avenger became insane. And then began that longing to reach the end of the world in search of the fugitives.

The mania of grandiosity had notable examples. The most remarkable was a poor fellow, the son of a water carrier, who narrated to the walls (because he never looked at any person) his entire genealogy, which went like this:

— God engendered an egg, the egg engendered the sword, the sword engendered David, David engendered the purple, the purple engendered the duke, the duke engendered the marquis, the marquis engendered the count, which is me.

He would hit his forehead, snap his fingers, and repeat five or six times in a row:

— God engendered an egg, the egg, etc.

Another of the same kind was a clerk who sold himself as the king's butler; another was a cattleman from Minas,[2] whose obsession was to distribute cattle to everyone, giving three hundred heads to one, six hundred to another, twelve hundred to another, and never stopping. I won't mention the cases of religious monomania; I'll just mention a guy named John of God who now claimed to be the god John, promising heaven to those who worshipped him and hell to the others. After him, there was licentiate Garcia, who said nothing because he imagined that on the day he uttered a single word, all the stars would detach from the sky and set the earth ablaze; such was the power he believed he had received from God.

This is what he wrote on the paper that the alienist had him sign, not out of charity but out of scientific interest.

. . . .

[2] [Minas Gerais, a Brazilian state.]

Simon Bacamarte, the alienist

Indeed, the patience of the alienist was even more extraordinary than all the manias hosted in Green House; nothing short of astonishing. Simon Bacamarte began by organizing an administrative staff, and accepting this idea from the apothecary Crispin Soares, he also accepted two nephews from him. He entrusted them with the execution of a set of regulations approved by the Council, involving the distribution of food and clothing, as well as handling administrative tasks, etc. It was the best he could do to focus solely on his profession. — Green House — he told the vicar — is now a kind of world with both temporal and spiritual governance. And Father Lopes chuckled at this pious exchange, adding with the sole purpose of making a joke, — Let it be, let it be, I will report you to the Pope.

Once relieved of the administration, the alienist proceeded to a vast classification of his patients. He first divided them into two main classes: the furious and the docile. He then moved on to subclasses, including monomanias, delusions, various hallucinations.

With this done, he began a detailed and continuous study. He analyzed the habits of each madman, the hours of onset, aversions, sympathies, words, gestures, tendencies; he inquired about the lives of the patients, their professions, customs, circumstances of morbid revelation, childhood and youth accidents, diseases of another kind, family antecedents, a thorough investigation, as would be conducted by the most astute magistrate. Each day brought a new observation, an interesting discovery, an extraordinary phenomenon. At the same time, he studied the best regimen, medicinal substances, curative and palliative measures, not only those found in his beloved Arab works but also those he discovered himself through wit and patience. Now, all this work consumed the better part of his time. He slept poorly and ate little; even while eating, it was as if he were working because he would either question an ancient text or ponder over a problem. Many times, he would go from one end of the meal to the other without saying a single word to Mrs. Evarista.

Chapter III: God Knows What He Does

Illustrious lady, at the end of two months, she found herself the most wretched of women: she fell into deep melancholy, became yellow, thin, ate little, and sighed at every turn. She dared not make any complaints or reproaches to him because she respected him as her husband and lord, but she suffered in silence and wasted away visibly. One day, at dinner, when her husband asked her what was wrong, she answered sadly that nothing was; then she ventured a little and went so far as to say that she considered herself as much a widow as before. And she added:

— Who would have thought that half a dozen lunatics…

She did not finish the sentence; or rather, she finished it by raising her eyes to the ceiling, — eyes, which were her most enticing feature, — black, large, bathed in a moist light, like the dawn. As for the gesture, it was the same as she had used on the day when Simon Bacamarte asked her to marry him. The chronicles do not say whether Mrs. Evarista brandished that weapon with the perverse intention of decapitating science at once, or at least cutting off its hands; but the conjecture is plausible. In any case, the alienist did not attribute any intention to her. And the great man did not get angry, not even dismayed. The metal of his eyes remained the same metal, hard, smooth, eternal, and the slightest wrinkle did not break the surface of the forehead as calm as the water of

Botafogo.[3] Perhaps a smile parted his lips, through which filtered this word as soft as the oil of the Canticle:

— I agree to let you take a trip to Rio de Janeiro.

Mrs. Evarista felt the ground beneath her feet disappear. Never had she seen Rio de Janeiro, which, although it was not even a pale shadow of what it is today, was still something more than Itaguai. Seeing Rio de Janeiro, for her, was equivalent to the dream of the captive Hebrew. Now, especially, since her husband had settled permanently in that countryside town, now that she had lost the last hopes of breathing the air of our good city; and precisely now he invited her to fulfill her desires of girlhood. Mrs. Evarista could not hide her delight at such a proposal. Simon Bacamarte paid her in advance and smiled, — a smile somewhat philosophical, as well as conjugal, in which seemed to be translated this thought: "There is no certain remedy for the pains of the soul; this lady languishes because it seems to her that I do not love her; I give her Rio de Janeiro, and she consoles herself." And because he was a studious man, he made a note of the observation.

But a dart pierced the heart of Mrs. Evarista. She restrained herself, however; she merely told her husband that if he was not going, she would not go either, because she wouldn't venture alone on the roads.

— You will go with your aunt. — retorted the alienist.

Note that Mrs. Evarista had thought of that very thing,

· · · · · · · ·

[3] [A neighborhood in the city of Rio de Janeiro.]

but she did not want to ask or hint at it, firstly because it would impose great expenses on her husband, secondly because it was better, more methodical, and rational for the proposal to come from him.

— Oh! But the money that will be necessary to spend! — sighed Mrs. Evarista without conviction.

— What does it matter? We have earned a lot, — said her husband. — Just yesterday, the clerk presented me with accounts. Do you want to see?

And he took her to the books. Mrs. Evarista was dazzled. It was a Milky Way of figures. And then he took her to the chests, where the money was.

God! There were mountains of gold, there were thousands of shillings upon thousands. of shillings, pence upon pence; it was opulence.

The gold of the alienist

While she devoured the gold with her black eyes, the alienist stared at her and whispered in her ear with the most perfidious of allusions:

— Who would have thought that half a dozen lunatics…

Mrs. Evarista understood, smiled, and replied with great resignation:

— God knows what He does!

Three months later, the journey took place. Mrs. Evarista, her aunt, the apothecary's wife, a nephew of his, a priest whom the alienist had known in Lisbon and happened to be in Itaguai, five or six pages, four maidservants, — such was the entourage that the population saw leaving one morning in May. The farewells were sad for everyone except the alienist. Although Mrs. Evarista's tears were abundant and sincere, they did not shake him. A man of science, and only of science, nothing outside of science distressed him; and if anything preoccupied him at that moment, if he cast an uneasy and police-like glance through the crowd, it was nothing more than the idea that some lunatic might be mixed with the sane people.

— Goodbye! — The ladies and the apothecary sobbed at last.

And the entourage departed. Crispin Soares, on his way back home, had his eyes between the two ears of the chestnut mare he was riding; Simon Bacamarte extended his over the horizon, leaving the responsibility of the return to the horse. Lively image of genius and ordinary! One gazes at the present, with all its tears and longing, the other examines the future with all its dawns.

Chapter IV: A New Theory

While Mrs. Evarista, in tears, was heading to Rio de Janeiro, Simon Bacamarte was exploring an audacious and new idea from all sides, one that could expand the foundations of psychology. All the time he had left from the cares of the Green House was barely enough for him to roam the streets or visit houses, engaging people in conversations on thirty thousand subjects, punctuating their speeches with a glance that struck fear into the most heroic individuals.

One morning, after three weeks had passed, while Crispin Soares was busy preparing a medication, they came to tell him that the alienist wanted him to come.

— It's about an important matter, as he told me. — added the messenger.

Crispin turned pale. What important matter could it be, if not some news about the entourage, especially his wife? Because this topic must be clearly defined, as the chroniclers insist on it: Crispin loved his wife, and for thirty years, they had never been separated for even a single day. This explains the monologues he was having now, which the servants often heard: — "Come on, well done, who told you to consent to Caesaria's trip? Sycophant, vile sycophant! Just to flatter Dr. Bacamarte. Well, now deal with it; come on, deal with it, lackey soul, weakling, vile, miserable. You say *amen* to everything, don't you? There you have the result, scoundrel!" — And many other ugly names that a man should not say to others, let alone to himself. To imagine the effect of the message is nothing.

As soon as he received it, he set aside the drugs and flew to the Green House.

Simon Bacamarte welcomed him with the joy characteristic of a sage, a joy buttoned up to the neck with circumspection.

— I am very pleased. — he said.

— News from our people? — asked the apothecary with a trembling voice.

The alienist made a magnificent gesture and replied:

— It's about something higher, it's about a scientific experiment. I say experiment because I dare not assure my idea right away; nor is science anything else, Mr. Soares, than a constant investigation. It is, therefore, an experiment, but an experiment that will change the face of the Earth. Madness, the object of my studies, was until now a lost island in the ocean of reason; I am beginning to suspect that it is a continent.

He said this and fell silent to let the apothecary digest his astonishment. Then he explained his idea at length. In his view, insanity covered a vast expanse of brains, and he developed this with a great wealth of reasoning, texts, and examples. He found examples in history and in Itaguai but, as a rare spirit that he was, he recognized the danger of citing all cases in Itaguai and took refuge in history. Thus, he particularly pointed out some famous characters, Socrates, who had a familiar demon, Pascal, who saw an abyss to the left, Muhammad, Caracalla, Domitian, Caligula, etc., a string of cases and people, in which odious and ridiculous entities were mixed. And because the apothecary was surprised by such a promiscuity, the alienist told him that it was all the same thing, and he even added sententiously:

— Ferocity, Mr. Soares, is serious grotesque.

— Witty, very witty! — Exclaimed Crispin Soares, raising his hands to the sky.

As for the idea of expanding the territory of madness, the apothecary found it extravagant, but his modesty, the main adornment of his spirit, did not allow him to confess anything other than noble enthusiasm; he declared it sublime and true and added that it was a "rattle case." This expression has no equivalent in modern style. At that time, Itaguai, like other villages, hamlets, and settlements in the colony, did not have a press, and there were two ways to disseminate news; either through handwritten posters posted on the door of the Chamber and the church, or through a rattle.

An old rattle

Here's what this second use consisted of. A man was hired for one or more days to walk the streets of the town with a rattle in his hand.

From time to time, he rang the rattle, gathered people, and announced what he was entrusted with: a remedy for fevers, plowed lands, a sonnet, a church donation, the best scissors in the village, the most beautiful speech of the year, etc. The system had drawbacks for public peace, but it was retained due to its great dissemination power. For example, one of the councilors — precisely the one who had opposed the creation of the Green House the most, — enjoyed the reputation of a perfect snake and monkey trainer, although he had never tamed any of these animals. He took care, however, to make the rattle works every month. And the chronicles say that some people claimed to have seen rattlesnakes dancing on the councilor's chest; a completely false assertion, but only due to the absolute confidence in the system. Truth be told, not all institutions of the old regime deserved the contempt of our century.

— There is something better than announcing my idea; it is to practice it. — replied the alienist to the apothecary's insinuation.

The apothecary, not significantly disagreeing with this view, told him that yes, it was better to start with the execution.

— There will always be time to give it to the rattle. — he concluded.

Simon Bacamarte reflected for a moment and said:

— I suppose the human mind is a vast shell. My goal, Mr. Soares, is to see if I can extract the pearl, which is reason; in other words, let's definitively demarcate the limits of reason and madness. Reason is the perfect balance of all faculties; beyond that, insanity, insanity, and only insanity.

The vicar Lopes, to whom he entrusted the new theory, frankly declared that he did not quite understand it, that it was an absurd work, and if it was not absurd, it was so colossal that it did not deserve to be put into practice.

— With the current definition, which is that of all times, — he added, — madness and reason are perfectly delimited. We know where one ends and the other begins. Why go beyond the fence?

On the thin and discreet lips of the alienist, there hovered the vague shadow of an intention to laugh, in which disdain was married to commiseration, but no word came out of his distinguished inner being.

Science contented itself with extending a hand to theology, — with such certainty that theology ultimately did not know whether to believe in itself or the other. Itaguai and the universe stood on the verge of a revolution.

Chapter V: The Terror

Four days later, the population of Itaguai heard with consternation the news that a certain Costa had been admitted to the Green House.

— Impossible!

— What do you mean impossible! He was admitted this morning.

— But, in truth, he did not deserve it… Right on top of everything! After all he did…

Costa was one of the most respected citizens of Itaguai. He had inherited four hundred thousand shillings in good currency from King Dom John V, money whose income was sufficient, as his uncle declared in the will, to live "until the end of the world." As soon as he received the inheritance, he began to divide it into loans without usury, a thousand shillings to one, two thousand to another, three hundred to this one, eight hundred to that one, to the point that, after five years, he had nothing left. If misery had come all at once, the astonishment in Itaguai would have been enormous, but it came slowly. He went from opulence to affluence, from affluence to mediocrity, from mediocrity to poverty, from poverty to misery, gradually.

After those five years, people who used to tip their hats when he appeared at the end of the street now patted him on the shoulder with familiarity, flicked his nose, said improper things to him. And Costa, always affable and smiling. He didn't seem to mind that the least courteous were precisely those who still owed him money. On the contrary, he seemed to welcome them with greater pleasure and more sublime resignation. One day, as one of these incurable debtors threw a coarse joke at him and he laughed it off, an ill-natured person remarked with a certain perfidy: "You put up with this guy to see if he'll pay you back." Costa didn't hesitate for a moment; he went to the debtor and forgave the debt. "No wonder," the other retorted, "Costa gave up a star that's in the sky." Costa was perceptive; he understood that the other denied all merit to the act, attributing to him the intention of rejecting what was not meant to be put in his pocket. He was also dignified and inventive; two hours later, he found a way to prove that such a stigma did not apply to him: he took some coins and lent them to the debtor.

— Now I hope that… — he thought, without finishing the sentence.

That last act by Costa convinced believers and skeptics alike; no one doubted the chivalrous sentiments of that worthy citizen anymore. The most modest needs took to the streets, came knocking on his door with their old slippers and patched capes. However, a worm gnawed at Costa's soul: the concept of the enemy. But even that ended; three months later, the enemy came to ask him for a hundred and twenty shillings with a promise to repay him within two days; it was the residue of the great inheritance, but it was also a noble revenge. Costa lent the money right away, and without interest. Unfortunately, he didn't have time to be repaid; five months later, he was admitted to the Green House.

One can imagine the consternation in Itaguai when they found out about the case. Nothing else was talked about; some said Costa went mad at lunch, others said it happened at dawn. They recounted the fits, which were either furious, dark, and terrible, — or gentle, and even funny, depending on the versions. Many people rushed to the Green House and found poor Costa, calm, a bit astonished, speaking very clearly, and asking why they had taken him there. Some went to see the alienist. Bacamarte approved these feelings of esteem and compassion, but added that science was science, and he could not leave a madman on the street. The last person who interceded for him (because after what I'm going to tell, no one dared to approach the dreaded doctor) was a poor lady, Costa's cousin. The alienist confidentially told her that this worthy man was not in perfect balance of mental faculties, considering how he had squandered the wealth that…

— No! No! Not that! — The good lady interrupted energetically. — If he spent what he received so quickly, it's not his fault.

— No?

— No, sir. I'll tell you how it happened. My late uncle was not a bad man, but when he was furious, he could even forget to tip his hat to the Blessed Sacrament. Now, one day, shortly before he died, he discovered that a slave had stolen a bull from him; imagine how he reacted. His face was a pepper; he trembled all over, his mouth frothing; I remember it as if it were today. Then a ugly, hairy man in a shirt approached him and asked for water. My uncle (may God rest his soul!) replied that he should go drink from the river or hell. The man looked at him, opened his hand threateningly, and cursed: "All your money will not last more than seven years and one day, as certain as this is the Solomon bell!" And he showed the Solomon bell printed on his arm. That's it, sir; it was this curse from that damned man.

Bacamarte fixed upon the poor lady a pair of eyes as sharp as daggers. When she finished, he extended his hand politely, as if he were doing so to the viceroy's own wife, and invited her to go speak to her cousin. The wretched woman believed him; he took her to the Green House and locked her in the gallery of the insane.

The news of this treacherous act by the illustrious Bacamarte struck terror into the hearts of the population. No one wanted to believe that, without reason, without enmity, the alienist would lock up in the Green House a perfectly sane lady who had no other crime than pleading for an unfortunate man. The case was discussed on street corners, in barber shops; a romance was constructed, with tender courtesies that the alienist had once directed at Costa's cousin, Costa's indignation, and the cousin's disdain. And from there, revenge. It was clear. But the severity of the alienist, the life of studies he led, seemed to contradict such a hypothesis. Stories! All of that was naturally the cover of a scoundrel. And one of the most credulous even murmured that he knew other things, he didn't say them because he wasn't completely sure, but he knew, almost could swear.

— You, who are close to him, couldn't you tell us what's going on, what happened, what the reason is…

Crispin Soares was overjoyed. This questioning from the restless and curious people, from the astonished friends, was a public consecration for him. There was no doubt; the whole town finally knew that the confidant of the alienist was him, Crispin, the apothecary, the collaborator of the great man and great things; hence the rush to the apothecary shop. All this was conveyed through the apothecary's cheerful face and his discreet laughter, laughter and silence, for he replied with nothing; one, two, three monosyllables at most, uttered, dry, capped by the faithful constant and small smile, full of scientific mysteries that he could not, without disgrace or danger, reveal to any human being.

— There's something. — thought the most suspicious ones.

One of these merely thought it, shrugged, and left. He had personal matters. He had just built a sumptuous house. The house alone was enough to attract everyone's attention; but there was more, — the furniture, which he had ordered from Hungary and the Netherlands, as he claimed, and which could be seen from outside because the windows were always open, — and the garden, a masterpiece of art and taste. This man, who had become rich in the saddle-making business, had always dreamed of a magnificent house, a grand garden, and rare furniture. He didn't leave the saddlery, but he found rest from it in the contemplation of the new house, the first in Itaguai, more magnificent than the Green House, nobler than the Town Hall. Among the illustrious people of the town, there were tears and gnashing of teeth when thinking, speaking, or praising the saddler's house, — a mere saddler, dear God!

— There he is, dumbfounded. — said the passersby, in the morning.

Indeed, in the morning, it was Matthew's custom to sprawl in the middle of the garden, with his eyes on the house, infatuated, for a long hour, until someone came to call him for lunch. The neighbors, although they greeted him with a certain respect, laughed behind his back, which he enjoyed. One of them even said that Matthew would be much more economical and would be very rich if he made the saddles for himself; an unintelligible epigram that caused uncontrollable laughter.

— Now there's Matthew being admired. — they said in the afternoon.

The reason for this other saying was that in the afternoon, when families went for a walk (they had dinner early), Matthew used to stand by the window, right in the center, showy, against a dark background, dressed in white, in a lordly attitude, and stayed like that for two or three hours until it got completely dark. It can be believed that Matthew's intention was to be admired and envied, although he confessed it to no one, neither to the apothecary nor to Father Lopes, his great friends. Nevertheless, this was the apothecary's argument when the alienist told him that the saddler might be suffering from the love of stones, a mania that Bacamarte had discovered and studied for some time. That business of contemplating the house…

— No, sir. — Crispin Soares vehemently interjected.

— No?

— Forgive me, but perhaps you don't know that in the morning he examines the work, he doesn't admire it; in the afternoon, others admire him and the work. — And he explained the saddler's habit, every afternoon, from early until nightfall.

A scientific pleasure illuminated Simon Bacamarte's eyes. Either he didn't know all the saddler's habits, or he only wanted to confirm some uncertain news or vague suspicion by questioning Crispin. The explanation satisfied him; but, as he had the joys proper to a sage, concentrated, the apothecary saw nothing that hinted at sinister intentions. On the contrary, it was in the afternoon, and the alienist asked him to accompany him for a walk. God! It was the first time Simon Bacamarte had honored his confidant with such a gesture; Crispin was trembling, bewildered, said yes, he was ready. Two or three people arrived from outside; Crispin mentally sent them all to hell; not only were they delaying the walk, but Bacamarte might choose one of them to accompany him and dismiss the apothecary. What an impatience! What an anguish!

Finally, they went out. The alienist led towards the saddler's house, saw him at the window, passed by five or six times slowly, stopping, examining the postures, the expression on his face. Poor Matthew, as soon as he noticed that he was the object of curiosity or admiration for Itaguai's foremost citizen, redoubled his expression, gave more emphasis to his postures… Sad! Unfortunately, he did nothing but condemn himself; the next day, he was taken to the Green House.

— The Green House is a private prison. — said a doctor without a practice.

Never has an opinion spread and flourished so rapidly. Private prison: that was what was repeated from north to south and from east to west of Itaguai, — albeit in fear, because during the week that followed the capture of poor Matthew, twenty-something people, — two or three of importance, — were taken to the Green House. The alienist claimed that only pathological cases were admitted, but few people believed him. Popular versions succeeded each other. Revenge, greed for money, God's punishment, the doctor's own monomania, a secret plan by Rio de Janeiro to destroy any germ of prosperity that might sprout, blossom, and flourish in Itaguai, with dishonor and diminution of that city, a thousand other explanations that explained nothing, such was the daily product of public imagination.

At this time, the wife of the alienist arrived from Rio de Janeiro, her aunt, Crispin Soares' wife, and the rest of the entourage, — or almost all, — that had left Itaguai a few weeks earlier. The alienist received her, with the apothecary, Father Lopes, the councilors, and several other magistrates. The moment when Mrs. Evarista set eyes on her husband is considered by the chroniclers of the time as one of the most sublime in the moral history of men, and this was due to the contrast of the two natures, both extreme, both eminent. Mrs. Evarista let out a cry, — stammered a word and threw herself at her spouse, — a gesture that can only be better defined by comparing it to a mixture of jaguar and dove. Not so the illustrious Bacamarte; as cold as a diagnosis, without for a moment losing the scientific rigidity, he extended his arms to the lady who fell into them and fainted. A brief incident; after two minutes, Mrs. Evarista received the congratulations of friends, and the procession set off.

Mrs. Evarista in Bacamarte's arms

Mrs. Evarista was Itaguai's hope; she was counted on to alleviate the scourge of the Green House. Hence the public acclamations, the immense crowd that filled the streets, the pennants, flowers, and damasks at the windows. With her arm leaning on Father Lopes', — because the eminent man had entrusted his wife to the vicar and accompanied them at a meditative pace, — Mrs. Evarista turned her head from side to side, curious, restless, and presumptuous. The vicar inquired about Rio de Janeiro, which he had not seen since the previous vice-reign; and Mrs. Evarista enthusiastically replied that it was the most beautiful thing that could exist in the world.

Rio de Janeiro at the time

The Public Walkway was finished, a paradise where she had often been, and the Street of the Beautiful Nights, the Ducks Fountain… Ah! The Ducks Fountain! They were really ducks — made of metal and spouting water from their mouths. A very gallant thing. The vicar agreed, saying that Rio de Janeiro must be even more beautiful now. If it already was in the past! It's no wonder, being larger than Itaguai, and moreover, the seat of the government. But it can't be said that Itaguai was ugly; it had beautiful houses, Matthew's house, the Green House…

— By the way, speaking of the Green House, — said Father Lopes skillfully sliding into the current topic, — you find it quite crowded.

— Really?

— It's true. There's Matthew…

— The saddler?

— The saddler; there's Costa, Costa's cousin, and so-and-so, and so-and-so…

— All of them crazy?

— Or almost crazy. — the priest replied.

— But why?

The vicar drooped the corners of his mouth, as if he didn't know anything or didn't want to say everything; a vague response that couldn't be repeated to someone else for lack of context. Mrs. Evarista found it truly extraordinary that all those people would go mad; one or two, fine; but everyone? However, she hesitated to doubt; her husband was a wise man; he wouldn't admit anyone to the Green House without clear evidence of madness.

— Without a doubt… without a doubt… — the vicar punctuated.

Three hours later, around fifty guests sat around Simon Bacamarte's table; it was the welcome dinner. Mrs.

Evarista was the obligatory subject of toasts, speeches, verses of all kinds, metaphors, amplifications, apologues. She was the wife of the new Hippocrates, the muse of science, an angel, divine, dawn, charity, life, consolation; she had two stars in her eyes, according to Crispin Soares' modest version, and two suns in the view of a councilor. The alienist listened to these things somewhat bored but without visible impatience. At most, he whispered to his wife that rhetoric allowed such meaningless extravagances. Mrs. Evarista made efforts to adhere to her husband's opinion; but even discounting three-quarters of the flattery, there was still plenty to inflate her soul. One of the speakers, for example, Martin Brito, a twenty-five-year-old guy, seasoned by love affairs and adventures, delivered a speech in which the birth of Mrs. Evarista was explained by the most singular of challenges.

— God, — he said, — after giving the universe to man and woman, this diamond and pearl of the divine crown, — and the speaker triumphantly dragged this phrase from one end of the table to the other, — God wanted to overcome God and created Mrs. Evarista.

Mrs. Evarista lowered her eyes with exemplary modesty. Two ladies, finding the flattery excessive and audacious, questioned the eyes of the host; and indeed, the gesture of the alienist seemed to them clouded with suspicions, threats, and probably blood. The audacity was great, thought the two ladies. And both prayed to God to remove any tragic episode — or at least to postpone it to the next day. Yes, to postpone it. One of them, the most pious, even admitted to herself that Mrs. Evarista deserved no suspicion, so far was she from being attractive or beautiful. Just a tepid water. The truth is that *if all tastes were the same, what would become of the color yellow*? This idea made her tremble again, although less; less, because the alienist was now smiling at Martin Brito, and, after everyone had risen, he went to him and spoke to him about the speech. He didn't deny that it was a brilliant improvisation, full of magnificent flashes. Was the idea regarding Mrs. Evarista's birth his own, or did he find it in some author who… No sir, it was his own; he came up with it on that occasion and it seemed suitable for an oratorical outburst. Moreover, his ideas were more daring than tender or humorous. They leaned towards the epic. Once, for example, he composed an ode to the fall of the Marquis of Pombal, in which he said that this minister was the "rugged dragoon of Nothing" crushed by the "avenging claws of the Whole"; and so on, more or less out of the ordinary; he liked sublime and rare ideas, grand and noble images…

— Poor boy! — Thought the alienist. And he continued to himself: — This is a case of brain injury: a phenomenon without gravity, but worthy of study…

Mrs. Evarista was stunned when she found out, three days later, that Martin Brito had been placed in the Green House. A young man with such beautiful ideas! The two ladies attributed the act to jealousy on the part of the alienist. It couldn't be anything else; indeed, the young man's declaration had been too audacious.

Jealousy? But how to explain that, shortly afterward, Joseph Borges of Couto Leme, an estimable person, Frank of the cambrics, a notorious jester, the clerk Fabricio, and several others were also taken in? The terror intensified. People no longer knew who was sane and who was mad. When husbands went safe, the wives would have a lamp lit for Our Lady; and not all husbands were valorous, some wouldn't venture out without one or two henchmen. Definitely terror. Those who could, emigrated. One of these fugitives was even arrested two hundred steps from the town. He was a thirty-year-old young man, amiable, talkative, polished — so polished that he wouldn't greet someone without doffing his hat to the ground; in the street, he would run a distance of ten to twenty yards to shake hands with a serious man, a lady, sometimes a child, as had happened to the son of the judge. He had the vocation of courtesy. Moreover, he owed his good relations in society not only to his rare personal qualities but also to the noble tenacity with which he never despaired in the face of one, two, four, six refusals, ugly faces, etc. What happened was that, once he entered a house, he never left it, nor did the people of the house leave him, so charming was Gil Bernardes. So, despite knowing he was esteemed, Gil Bernardes became frightened when someone told him one day that the alienist had an eye on him; the next dawn, he fled the town, but was soon caught and taken to the Green House.

— We must put an end to this!!

— It can't go on!

— Down with tyranny!!

— Despot! Violent! Goliath!

It wasn't shouts in the streets; it was sighs at home, but the time for shouts was not far off. The terror grew; rebellion was approaching. The idea of a petition to the government to have Simon Bacamarte captured and deported crossed some minds before the barber Porphyry expressed it in his shop with great gestures of indignation. Note, — and this is one of the purest pages of this dark story, — note that Porphyry, since the Green House began to be populated so extraordinarily, saw his profits increase due to the frequent application of leeches requested from there; but personal interest, he said, must yield to public interest. And he added: — We must overthrow the tyrant! — Note also that he shouted this on the very day Simon Bacamarte had a man brought to the Green House who had a lawsuit with him, Coelho.

— Can't you tell me how Coelho is crazy? — Porphyry shouted.

And no one answered him; everyone repeated that he was perfectly sane. The same lawsuit he brought with the barber, about some lands in the town, was born from the obscurity of a decree and not from greed or hatred. Coelho was an excellent character. The only ones who disliked him were some individuals who, claiming to be taciturn or pretending to be in a hurry, as soon as they saw him from a distance would turn corners, enter shops, etc. Indeed, he loved good conversation, lengthy conversation, relished in large sips, and that's why he was never alone, preferring those who knew how to say two words but not despising the others. Father Lopes, who studied Dante and was an enemy of Coelho, never saw him separate from someone who didn't recite and emend this passage:

> *La bocca sollevò dal fiero pasto*
> *Quel "seccatore"...* [4]

but some knew about the priest's hatred, and others thought this was a prayer in Latin.

·······

[4] "The mouth lifted from the fierce repast that sinner..." — Dante Alighieri, in the work *The Divine Comedy*.

Chapter VI: The Rebellion

About thirty people joined the barber, drafted, and took a petition to the City Council.

The City Council refused to accept it, declaring that Green House was a public institution, and that science could not be amended by administrative vote, much less by street movements.

— Return to work, — concluded the president, — that is the advice we give you.

The agitation of the protesters was enormous. The barber declared that they would raise the banner of rebellion and destroy Green House; that Itaguai could not continue to serve as a corpse for the studies and experiments of a despot; that many estimable and some distinguished individuals, others humble but worthy of respect, lay in the cubicles of Green House; that the scientific despotism of the alienist was compounded by the spirit of greed, since the madmen or supposed ones were not treated for free: families, and in their absence, the City Council paid the alienist...

— It's false! — Interrupted the president.

— False?

— About two weeks ago, we received a letter from the illustrious doctor in which he declares that, in seeking to carry out experiments of high psychological value, he renounces the stipend voted by the City Council, as well as anything he would receive from the families of the patients.

The news of this noble, pure act somewhat suspended the souls of the rebels. Surely, the alienist could be mistaken, but no interest other than science instigated him; and to demonstrate the error, something more than disturbances and clamors was needed. This was stated by the president, to the applause of the entire City Council. The barber, after a few moments of concentration, declared that he was invested with a public mandate and would not restore peace to Itaguai until he saw Green House demolished — "Bastille of human reason" — an expression he heard from a local poet and repeated with great emphasis. He said this, and, with a signal, everyone left with him.

Imagine the situation of the councilors; it was urgent to prevent the assembly, the rebellion, the struggle, the bloodshed. To add to the problem, one of the councilors who had supported the president, now hearing the term given by the barber to Green House — "Bastille of human reason" — found it so elegant that he changed his mind. He said that it seemed prudent to decree some measure to reduce Green House; and because the president, indignant, expressed his astonishment in vigorous terms, the councilor made this reflection:

— I have nothing to do with science; but if so many men whom we think are sane are confined as lunatics, who assures us that the alienated one is not the alienist?

Sebastian Freitas, the dissenting councilor, had the gift of speech and spoke for some time, with prudence but with firmness. His colleagues were astonished; the president asked him, at least, to set an example of order and respect for the law, not to vent his ideas in the street so as not to give substance and soul to the rebellion, which was for now a whirlwind of scattered atoms. This figure corrected the effect of the other somewhat: Sebastian Freitas promised to suspend any action, reserving the right to seek through legal means the reduction of Green House. And he repeated to himself, infatuated: — Bastille of human reason!

Councilors debating

Meanwhile, the commotion was growing. There were no longer thirty but three hundred people following the barber, whose familiar nickname must be mentioned because it gave its name to the revolt; they called him Canjica,[5] — and the movement became famous under the name of the Canjicas' revolt. The action could be restricted, — since many people, either out of fear or out of habits of education, did not go down to the street; but the

. . . .

[5] [A traditional Brazilian dish made with maize.]

sentiment was unanimous, or almost unanimous, and the three hundred who were marching towards Green House, — given the difference from Paris to Itaguai, — could be compared to those who took the Bastille.

Hundreds of people marching towards the Green House

Mrs. Evarista had news of the rebellion before it arrived; one of her servants came to inform her. At that moment, she was trying on a silk dress, — one of the thirty-seven she had brought from Rio de Janeiro, — and did not want to believe it.

— It must be some jest, — she said, changing the position of a pin. — Benedicta, see if the hem is good.

— It is, ma'am, — replied the maid squatting on the floor, — it's good. Ma'am, take a look for a moment. Like this. It's very good.

— It's not a jest, ma'am; they're shouting: — Death to Dr. Bacamarte!!! the tyrant! — said the frightened boy.

— Shut up, fool! Benedicta, look on the left side there; doesn't it seem that the seam is a little skewed? The blue line doesn't go all the way down; it looks very ugly like this; it needs to be unstitched to make it look exactly the same and…

— Death to Dr. Bacamarte!!! Death to the tyrant! — Three hundred voices howled outside. It was the rebellion pouring into New Street.

Mrs. Evarista turned pale. Initially, she didn't move or make a gesture; terror petrified her. The maid instinctively ran to the back door. As for the boy, whom Mrs. Evarista hadn't believed, he had an instant of sudden, imperceptible, profound moral triumph at seeing reality swear by him.

— Death to the alienist! — shouted voices closer now.

Mrs. Evarista, if she didn't easily resist moments of pleasure, knew how to face moments of danger. She didn't faint; she rushed into the inner room where her husband was studying. When she entered, hurried, the illustrious doctor was scrutinizing a text by Averroes; his eyes, clouded by contemplation, moved from the book to the manuscript and lowered from the manuscript to the book, blind to the external reality, seeing into the depths of mental work. Mrs. Evarista called her husband twice without him paying attention; at the third call, he listened and asked her what was wrong, if she was sick.

— Can't you hear those shouts? — asked the worthy wife in tears.

The alienist then paid attention; the shouts were approaching, terrifying, threatening; he understood everything. He rose from the high-backed chair he was sitting on, closed the book, and, with a firm and calm step, went to place it on the shelf. As the introduction of the volume disturbed the alignment of the two adjacent volumes a little, Simon Bacamarte took care to correct this minor, and otherwise interesting, defect. Then he told his wife to retire, not to do anything.

— No, no, — pleaded the worthy lady, — I want to die by your side…

Simon Bacamarte insisted that it was not a case of death; and even if it were, he urged her, in the name of life, to stay. The unfortunate lady bowed her head, obedient and tearful.

— Down with the Green House! — shouted the Canjicas.

The alienist walked towards the front balcony and arrived just as the rebellion also arrived and stopped, facing him, with its three hundred heads shining with civic duty and shaded by despair. — Die! Die! — They shouted from all sides, as soon as the figure of the alienist appeared on the balcony. Simon Bacamarte gestured to speak; the rebels drowned his voice with shouts of indignation. Then the barber, waving his hat to impose silence on the crowd, managed to calm his friends and declared to the alienist that he could speak, but added that he shouldn't abuse the people's patience as he had done so far.

— I will say little, or even nothing, if necessary. I wish to know first what you demand.

— We demand nothing, — replied the barber, trembling; — we order that the Green House be demolished, or at least stripped of the wretches who are there.

— I don't understand.

— You understand well, tyrant; we want to give freedom to the victims of your hatred, caprice, greed…

The alienist smiled, but the smile of this great man was not something visible to the eyes of the crowd; it was a slight contraction of two or three muscles, nothing more. He smiled and replied:

— Gentlemen, science is a serious matter and deserves to be treated seriously. I don't justify my acts as an alienist to anyone, except to my teachers and to God. If you want to improve the administration of the Green House, I am ready to listen to you; but if you demand that I deny myself, you will gain nothing. I could invite some of you as representatives of the others to come and see the confined lunatics with me, but I won't do it because it would be giving you justification for my system, which I won't do for laymen or rebels.

The alienist said this, and the crowd was astonished; it was clear that they did not expect so much energy and even less such composure. But the amazement reached its peak when the alienist, bowing to the crowd very gravely, turned his back and withdrew slowly inside. The barber quickly came to himself and, waving his hat, invited his friends to demolish the Green House; few and weak voices responded. It was in this decisive moment that the barber felt the ambition for power emerging within him; it seemed to him that by demolishing the Green House and overthrowing the influence of the alienist, he could seize control of the City Council, dominate the other authorities, and become the master of Itaguai. For some years, he had been striving to have his name included in the lots for the selection of councilors, but he was rejected for not having a position compatible with such a high office. The opportunity was now or never. Moreover, he had gone so far in the riot that defeat would mean imprisonment or perhaps the gallows or exile. Unfortunately, the alienist's response had diminished the fury of his followers. The barber, as soon as he realized it, felt an impulse of indignation and wanted to shout at them: — Rascals! Cowards! — but he restrained himself and burst out like this:

— My friends, let us fight to the end! The salvation of Itaguai is in your worthy and heroic hands. Let us destroy the prison of your sons and fathers, your mothers and sisters, your relatives and friends, and yourselves. Or you will die on bread and water, perhaps by the whip, in the dungeon of that unworthy man.

And the crowd stirred, murmured, shouted, threatened, all gathered around the barber. It was the revolt regaining consciousness from its brief swoon and threatening to raze the Green House.

— Let's go! — shouted Porphyry, waving his hat.

— Let's go! — everyone repeated.

They were stopped by an incident: it was a corps of dragoons that, marching, entered New Street.

Corps of dragoons

Chapter VII: The Unexpected

When the dragoons arrived in front of the Canjicas, there was a moment of astonishment. The Canjicas could not believe that the police force was sent against them, but the barber understood everything and waited. The dragoons stopped, the captain ordered the crowd to disperse; however, although a part of it was inclined to do so, the other part strongly supported the barber, whose response consisted of these elevated terms:

— We will not disperse. If you want our corpses, you can take them, but only the corpses; you will not take our honor, our credit, our rights, and with them, the salvation of Itaguai.

Nothing was more imprudent than this response from the barber, and nothing was more natural. It was the vertigo of great crises. Perhaps it was also an excess of confidence in the restraint of arms on the part of the dragoons; a confidence that the captain immediately dispelled by ordering a charge against the Canjicas. The moment was indescribable. The crowd roared furiously; some, climbing to the windows of houses or running down the street, managed to escape; but the majority remained fuming with anger, outraged, inspired by the barber's exhortation. The defeat of the Canjicas was imminent when a third of the dragoons — whatever the reason, the chronicles do not declare — suddenly switched sides to join the rebellion. This unexpected reinforcement revived the spirits of the Canjicas while casting discouragement into the ranks of legality. The loyal soldiers did not have the courage to attack their own comrades, and one by one, they went over to them, so that, after a few minutes, the aspect of things was completely different. The captain was on one side with some people against a compact mass threatening him with death. He had no choice but to declare himself defeated and handed his sword to the barber.

The victorious revolution did not lose a minute; they took the wounded to nearby houses and led the People and troops to the City Council. People and troops fraternized, cheering for the King, the Viceroy, Itaguai, and the "illustrious Porphyry." The latter was at the forefront, wielding the sword so skillfully, as if it were merely a slightly longer razor. Victory crowned his forehead with a mysterious halo. The dignity of government was beginning to stiffen his hips.

The councilors, from the windows, seeing the crowd and the troops, thought that the troops had captured the crowd, and without further examination, they entered and voted a petition to the Viceroy to grant a month's pay to the dragoons, "whose bravery saved Itaguai from the abyss to which a gang of rebels had thrown it." This phrase was proposed by Sebastian Freitas, the dissenting councilor whose defense of the Canjicas had scandalized his colleagues. But the illusion quickly dissipated. Cheers for the barber, curses for the councilors and the alienist came to inform them of the sad reality. The president did not lose heart: "Whatever our fate, let us remember that we are in the service of His Majesty and the people." Sebastian hinted that one could better serve the crown and the town by slipping out the back and going to confer with the judge from outside, but the entire Council rejected this advice.

Before long, the barber, accompanied by some of his lieutenants, entered the council chamber and demanded the fall of the Council. The Council did not resist, surrendered, and went from there to jail. Then the barber's friends suggested that he should assume the government of the town in the name of His Majesty. Porphyry accepted the task, although he acknowledged (he added) the thorns it brought; he also said that he could not do without the support of the present friends, to which they promptly agreed. The barber came to the window and communicated these resolutions to the people, which the people ratified, acclaiming the barber. He took the title of "Protector of the town in the name of His Majesty and the people." Several important orders were immediately issued, official communications from the new government, a detailed report to the Viceroy, with many protests of obedience to His Majesty's orders; finally, a proclamation to the people, short but forceful:

"People from Itaguai!

A corrupt and violent Council conspired against the interests of His Majesty and the people. Public opinion had condemned it; a handful of citizens, strongly supported by the brave dragoons of His Majesty, has just ignominiously dissolved it, and by unanimous consent of the town, supreme command has been entrusted to me until His Majesty sees fit to order what seems best for his royal service. People from Itaguai! I ask nothing more than that you surround me with trust, assist me in restoring peace and public affairs, so recklessly squandered by the Council that has now ended in your hands. Count on my sacrifice, and rest assured that the crown will be for us.

The Protector of the town in the name of His Majesty and the people

PORPHYRY CAETANO OF NEVES."

Everyone noticed the absolute silence of this proclamation regarding the Green House, and according to some, there could be no more vivid indication of the barber's dark plans. The danger was even greater because, in the midst of these serious events, the alienist had placed about seven or eight people in the Green House, including two ladies, and one of the men was related to the Protector. It was not a challenge, not an intentional act, but everyone interpreted it that way; and the town breathed with hope that the alienist would be in chains within twenty-four hours, and the dreaded prison would be destroyed.

The day ended joyfully. While the town crier was reciting the proclamation from corner to corner, the people scattered in the streets and pledged to die in defense of the illustrious Porphyry. Few shouts against the Green House, a sign of confidence in the government's actions. The barber issued a decree declaring that day a holiday and entered into negotiations with the vicar for the celebration of a *Te Deum*,[6] as the conjunction of temporal power with spiritual power was so convenient in his eyes. However, Father Lopes openly refused his concourse.

— In any case, Your Reverence will not align yourself with the enemies of the government? — the barber asked, giving his face a sinister look.

To which Father Lopes replied, without really answering:

— How can I align myself if the new government has no enemies?

The barber smiled; it was the plain truth. Except for the captain, the councilors, and the town's leaders, everyone acclaimed him. Even the leaders, if they did not acclaim him, had not risen against him. None of the constables failed to come to receive his orders. Overall, families blessed the name of the man who was finally going to free Itaguai from the Green House and the terrible Simon Bacamarte.

· · · · · · ·

[6] [*Traditional prayer among Catholics.*]

Chapter VIII: The Apothecary's Agonies

Twenty-four hours after the events narrated in the previous chapter, the barber left the government palace — this was the name given to the Town Council's house — with two aides-de-camp and headed to Simon Bacamarte's residence. He was aware that it would be more decorous for the government to summon him; however, the fear that the alienist might not obey forced him to appear tolerant and moderate.

I do not describe the terror of the apothecary upon hearing that the barber was going to the alienist's house. — He's going to arrest him, — he thought. And his anguishes redoubled. Indeed, the moral torture of the apothecary in those days of revolution exceeds all possible description. Never has a man been in a tighter spot: — the intimacy with the alienist called him to the latter's side, while the victory of the barber drew him to the barber. The mere news of the uprising had already shaken his soul vigorously because he knew the unanimity of the hatred against the alienist. However, the final victory was also the final blow. His wife, a masculine lady and a particular friend of Mrs. Evarista, said that his place was by Simon Bacamarte's side, while his heart shouted that no, the alienist's cause was lost, and no one ties themselves to a corpse by their own act. Cato did it, indeed, *sed victa Catoni*[7], he thought, recalling some habitual talks of Father Lopes; but Cato did not tie himself to a lost cause, he was the lost cause, the cause of the republic; therefore,

· · · · · · ·

[7] "But for Cato, the cause was lost" — Latin quotation.

his act was selfish, that of a miserable egoist; my situation is different.

However, when his wife insisted, Crispin Soares found no other way out of such a crisis than to fall ill; he declared himself sick and took to bed.

— There goes Porphyry to Dr. Bacamarte's house, — his wife told him the next day by his bedside; — he's accompanied by a crowd.

— He's going to arrest him. — thought the apothecary.

One idea leads to another; the apothecary imagined that once the alienist was arrested, they would also come to get him as an accomplice. This idea was the best of vesicants. Crispin Soares got up, said he was well, that he was going out; and despite all the efforts and protests of his consort, he dressed and went out. The old chroniclers unanimously say that the certainty that her husband was nobly placing himself by the alienist's side greatly comforted the apothecary's wife; and with keen insight, they note the immense moral power of an illusion. The apothecary walked resolutely to the government palace and not to the alienist's house. Upon arriving there, he expressed surprise at not seeing the barber, to whom he intended to present his protests of adherence, not having done so since the day before due to illness. And he coughed with some difficulty. The high officials who heard this declaration, aware of the apothecary's intimacy with the alienist, understood the full importance of the new adherence and treated Crispin Soares with refined affection; they assured him that the barber was not far behind, His Lordship had gone to the Green House for an important matter but would not be long. They gave him a chair, refreshments, compliments; they told him that the cause of the illustrious Porphyry was that of all patriots; to which the apothecary kept repeating yes, that he had never thought otherwise, that he would declare that to His Majesty himself.

Porphyry the barber

Chapter IX: Two Beautiful Cases

The alienist did not delay in receiving the barber; he declared that he had no means of resisting and, therefore, was ready to obey. He only requested one thing: not to be forced to personally witness the destruction of the Green House.

— You are mistaken, Your Lordship, — said the barber after a pause, — you are mistaken in attributing vandal intentions to the government. Rightly or wrongly, public opinion believes that most of the madmen placed there are in their right minds, but the government recognizes that the issue is purely scientific and has no intention of resolving scientific issues through ordinances… Furthermore, the Green House is a public institution; we accepted it as such from the dissolved Council. However, there must be some intermediate solution that restores public tranquility.

The alienist could hardly conceal his astonishment; he confessed that he expected something else: the demolition of the asylum, his arrest, exile, everything, except…

— The amazement of Your Lordship, — the barber gravely interrupted, — comes from not considering the serious responsibility of the government. The people, driven by a blind piety that legitimately gives rise to indignation in such cases, may demand certain acts from the government, but with the responsibility it bears, it should not carry them out, at least not in full. Such is our situation. The generous revolution that yesterday overthrew a vilified and corrupt Council loudly demanded the demolition of the Green House, but can the government eradicate madness? No. And if the government cannot eliminate it, is it at least able to discriminate it, recognize it? No, it is a matter of science. Therefore, in such a delicate matter, the government cannot, and does not want to, dispense with Your Lordship's cooperation. What it asks is that we somehow provide some satisfaction to the people. Let us unite, and the people will know how to obey. One of the acceptable suggestions, if Your Lordship does not propose another, would be to remove from the Green House those patients who are almost cured and also the minor maniacs, etc. In this way, without great danger, we will show some tolerance and benevolence.

— How many dead and wounded were there in yesterday's conflict? — Simon Bacamarte asked after about three minutes.

The barber was surprised by the question but immediately answered that there were eleven dead and twenty-five wounded.

— Eleven dead and twenty-five wounded! — repeated the alienist two or three times.

He then declared that the suggestion did not seem good to him, but that he would find some other solution, and within a few days, he would provide an answer. He asked several questions about the events of the previous day, the attack, defense, the support of the dragoons, the resistance of the Council, etc. The barber responded abundantly, emphasizing the discredit that had befallen the Council. The barber admitted that the new government did not yet have the trust of the town's leading figures, but the alienist could play a significant role in this regard. The government, the barber concluded, would be delighted if it could count not only on the sympathy but on the benevolence of the highest intellect in Itaguai and, assuredly, the kingdom. However, none of this altered the noble and austere countenance of that great man who listened silently, without conceit or modesty, but impassive like a stone god.

— Eleven dead and twenty-five wounded, — repeated the alienist after accompanying the barber to the door. — Here are two beautiful cases of cerebral illness. The symptoms of duplicity and shamelessness in this barber are evident. As for the madness of those who hailed him, no further proof is needed than the eleven dead and twenty-five wounded. Two beautiful cases!

— Long live the illustrious Porphyry! — shouted about thirty people who were waiting for the barber at the door.

The alienist peeked through the window and still heard the end of a short speech from the barber to the thirty people who were cheering him.

— … because I assure you, you can be certain of it, I ensure the execution of the people's will. Trust me, and everything will be done in the best way. I only recommend order. And order, my friends, is the foundation of government…

— Long live the illustrious Porphyry! — shouted the thirty voices, waving their hats.

— Two beautiful cases! — murmured the alienist.

Chapter X: Restoration

Within five days, the alienist admitted around fifty supporters of the new government to the Green House. The people were outraged. The government, bewildered, didn't know how to react. John Pina, another barber, openly stated in the streets that Porphyry was "sold to Simon Bacamarte's gold," a phrase that rallied the most determined people in the town around John Pina. Porphyry, seeing his old rival leading the uprising, understood that his loss was irreparable if he didn't make a bold move. He issued two decrees, one abolishing the Green House, and another banishing the alienist. John Pina made it clear with grand phrases that Porphyry's act was a mere spectacle, a deception that the people shouldn't believe. Two hours later, Porphyry fell ignominiously, and John Pina took on the challenging task of government. Finding drafts of proclamations, statements to the viceroy, and other inaugural acts of the previous government in the drawers, he hurried to have them copied and dispatched. The chroniclers add, and it is otherwise implied, that he changed their names, and where the other barber had spoken of a corrupt Council, this one spoke of "an intruder tainted with bad French doctrines and contrary to the sacred interests of His Majesty," etc.

At this point, a force sent by the viceroy entered the town and restored order. The alienist immediately demanded the surrender of barber Porphyry and also of about fifty individuals he declared mentally disturbed. Not only did they hand over these individuals, but they also assured him of delivering nineteen more followers of the barber who were recovering from wounds sustained in the first rebellion.

This moment in the crisis of Itaguai also marks the peak of Simon Bacamarte's influence. Everything he wanted was granted to him. One of the most vivid proofs of the illustrious doctor's power is seen in the readiness with which the councilors, reinstated in their positions, agreed to have Sebastian Freitas also admitted to the asylum. The alienist, aware of the extraordinary inconsistency of this councilor's opinions, deemed it a pathological case and requested him. The same fate befell the apothecary. As soon as they informed the alienist of Crispin Soares' momentary support for the Canjicas' rebellion, he compared it to the approval he had always received from him even the day before and ordered his capture. Crispin Soares did not deny the fact but explained it by saying that he succumbed to a movement of terror upon seeing the triumphant rebellion and used the absence of any other action on his part as proof, adding that he promptly returned to bed, claiming illness. Simon Bacamarte did not contradict him but told those present that terror is also the father of madness and that Crispin Soares' case seemed to him one of the most characteristic.

But the most evident proof of Simon Bacamarte's influence was the docility with which the Council handed over its own president to him. This worthy magistrate had declared in a full session that he would not be satisfied, to wash off the Canjicas' affront, with less than seven hundred liters of blood, a word that reached the alienist's ears through the enthusiastic secretary of the Council. Simon Bacamarte began by admitting the secretary to the Green House and then went to the Council, where he declared that the president was suffering from the "madness of bulls," a genre he intended to study with great advantage to the people. The Council hesitated at first but eventually gave in.

From then on, it was an unrestrained collection. A man could not give birth to or propagate the simplest lie in the world, even those that benefited the inventor or propagator, without being immediately admitted to the Green House. Everything was considered madness. Enigma enthusiasts, makers of charades and anagrams, gossipers, busybodies, the overly proud constable, no one escaped the emissaries of the alienist. He respected girlfriends but did not spare flirts, stating that the former yielded to a natural impulse and the latter to a vice. If a man was miserly or prodigal, he would similarly end up in the Green House; hence the claim that there was no rule for complete mental sanity. Some chroniclers believe that Simon Bacamarte did not always act with fairness and cite in support of the assertion (whose acceptance I do not know) the fact that he obtained a Council decree authorizing the wearing of a silver ring on the thumb of the left hand by anyone who, without other documentary or traditional proof, declared to have two or three ounces of Gothic blood in their veins. These chroniclers say that the secret purpose of the suggestion to the Council was to enrich a jeweler friend and godfather of his. Still, although it is true that the jeweler saw his business prosper after the new municipal ordinance, it is equally true that this decree brought a multitude of tenants to the Green House. Therefore, one cannot define, without temerity, the true purpose of the illustrious doctor. As for the determining reason for the capture and retirement to the Green House of all those who wore the ring, it is one of the darkest points in the history of Itaguai. The most plausible opinion is that they were admitted because they gestured too much, praising, in the streets, at home, in the church. It is well known that madmen gesture a lot. In any case, it is a mere conjecture; there is nothing certain.

— Where is this man going to end up? — said the town's dignitaries. — Ah! If we had supported the Canjicas…

One morning, — on a day when the Council was supposed to host a grand ball, — the entire town was shaken by the news that the alienist's own wife had been admitted to the Green House. No one believed it; it must be the invention of some mischievous youngster. But it wasn't; it was pure truth. Mrs. Evarista had been admitted at two in the morning. Father Lopes rushed to the alienist and discreetly questioned him about the incident.

— I had suspected for some time. — the husband said gravely. — The modesty with which she lived through both marriages could not reconcile with the fervor for silks, velvets, lace, and precious stones that she exhibited upon returning from Rio de Janeiro. Since then, I began to observe her. All her conversations revolved around these objects; if I spoke to her about ancient courts, she immediately inquired about the fashion of the ladies' dresses. If a lady visited her in my absence, before telling me the purpose of the visit, she described the attire, approving some things and criticizing others. One day, I believe Your Reverence will remember, she proposed to annually make a dress for the image of Our Lady at the church. All these were grave symptoms; tonight, however, total dementia declared itself. She had chosen, prepared, and adorned the dress she would wear to the Council's ball; she only hesitated between a garnet necklace and a sapphire one. The night before last, she asked me which one to wear; I told her that either suited her well. Yesterday she repeated the question at lunch; shortly after dinner, I found her silent and pensive. — What's wrong? — I asked her. — I want to wear the garnet necklace, but I find the sapphire one so beautiful! — Well, wear the sapphire one. — Ah! But where is the garnet one? — Finally, the evening passed without incident. We had supper and went to bed. Late at night, around one and a half hours, I woke up and didn't see her; I got up, went to the dressing room, found her in front of the two necklaces, trying them on in front of the mirror, now one, now the other. Dementia was evident: I admitted her right away.

Father Lopes was not satisfied with the answer but did not object. The alienist, however, perceived it and explained to him that Mrs. Evarista's case was a "saintly mania," not incurable, and in any case worthy of study.

Mrs. Evarista trying jewels

— I expect to have her well within six weeks. — he concluded.

The illustrious doctor's selflessness added great luster to his reputation. Speculations, inventions, suspicions, everything fell apart since he did not hesitate to admit his own wife to the Green House, whom he loved with all the strength of his soul. No one else had the right to resist him — much less to attribute intentions other than science to him.

He was a great and austere man, a Hippocrates clad in Cato.

Chapter XI: The Astonishment of Itaguai

And now, let the reader prepare for the same astonishment that befell the town one day upon knowing that the madmen from the Green House were all going to be released.

— All of them?

— All of them.

— It's impossible; some, yes, but all of them…

— All. That's what he said in the letter he sent to the Council this morning.

The letter of Simon Bacamarte

Indeed, the alienist had written to the Council stating: 1) that he had verified from the town and Green House statistics that four-fifths of the population were housed in that establishment; 2) that this population displacement led him to examine the foundations of his theory of brain diseases, a theory that excluded from reason all cases where the balance of faculties was not perfect and absolute; 3) that, from this examination and the statistical fact, he had become convinced that the true doctrine was not that one but the opposite, and therefore, it should be admitted as normal and exemplary to have an imbalance of faculties, and as pathological hypotheses all cases in which that balance was uninterrupted; 4) that, in view of this, he declared to the Council that he was going to grant freedom to the inmates of Green House and accommodate in it the people who were now in the conditions outlined; 5) that, in seeking to discover the scientific truth, he would spare no efforts of any kind, hoping for equal dedication from the Council; 6) that he was returning to the Council and individuals the sum received for the accommodation of the alleged madmen, deducting the portion effectively spent on food, clothing, etc.; which the Council would have to verify in the books and chests of Green House.

The astonishment in Itaguai was great; no less was the joy of the relatives and friends of the inmates. Dinners, dances, luminaires, music, everything happened to celebrate such a momentous event. I won't describe the celebrations as they are not relevant to our purpose, but they were splendid, touching, and prolonged.

And so go human affairs! In the midst of the rejoicing caused by Simon Bacamarte's letter, no one noticed the final sentence in paragraph 4, a sentence full of future experiments.

Chapter XII: The End of Paragraph 4

The luminaires were extinguished, families were reunited, everything seemed to be restored to its former state. Order prevailed, the Council once again exercised government without any external pressure; the president and the councilor Freitas returned to their positions. The barber Porphyry, taught by events, having "tried everything," as the poet said of Napoleon, and a little more, because Napoleon did not experience Green House, the barber found the obscure glory of the razor and scissors preferable to the brilliant calamities of power; he was indeed prosecuted, but the town's population implored His Majesty's clemency, hence the pardon. John Pina was acquitted, considering that he had overthrown a rebel. Chroniclers believe that this event gave rise to our proverb: — "A thief who steals from another thief has a hundred years of pardon"; — an immoral proverb, it's true, but greatly useful.

Not only did complaints against the alienist cease, but no resentment remained for the acts he had committed; moreover, the inmates of Green House, since he declared them fully sane, felt a deep sense of gratitude and fervent enthusiasm. Many believed that the alienist deserved a special manifestation and threw a ball in his honor, followed by other balls and dinners. Chronicles say that Mrs. Evarista initially thought of separating from her husband, but the pain of losing the company of such a great man overcame any resentment of self-love, and the couple became even happier than before.

The friendship between the alienist and the apothecary remained no less intimate. The apothecary concluded from Simon Bacamarte's letter that prudence is the first of virtues in times of revolution and greatly appreciated the magnanimity of the alienist, who, in granting him freedom, extended the hand of an old friend.

— He is a great man. — he told his wife, referring to that circumstance.

There is no need to talk about the saddler, Costa, Coelho, Martin Brito, and others specifically named in this narrative; it suffices to say that they were able to freely resume their previous habits. Martin Brito himself, confined for a speech in which he praised Mrs. Evarista emphatically, now made another in honor of the eminent doctor, — "whose lofty genius, soaring his wings far above the sun, left all other spirits of the earth below him."

— I thank you for your words, — replied the alienist, — and I do not regret having restored you to freedom.

However, the Council, which had responded to Simon Bacamarte's letter with the reservation that it would legislate on the paragraph 4 in due course, finally legislated on it. A decree was adored without debate, authorizing the alienist to shelter in Green House those individuals who enjoyed perfect mental faculties. And because the Council's experience had been painful, it established the clause that the authorization was provisional, limited to one year, for the purpose of testing the new psychological theory, and the Council could, even before that period, order the closure of Green House if advised by reasons of public order. Councilor Freitas also proposed a declaration that, under no circumstances, should councilors be admitted to the asylum for the insane: a clause that was accepted, voted on, and included in the decree despite objections from councilor Galvan. The main argument of this magistrate was that the Council, legislating on a scientific experiment, could not exempt its members from the consequences of the law; the exception was odious and ridiculous. As soon as he uttered these two words, the councilors erupted in loud exclamations against the audacity and foolishness of their colleague; however, he listened to them and merely stated that he voted against the exception.

— The Council, — he concluded, — gives us no special power and does not eliminate us from the human spirit.

Simon Bacamarte accepted the decree with all the restrictions. Regarding the exclusion of councilors, he declared that he would feel deep regret if compelled to admit them to Green House; however, the clause was the best proof that they did not suffer from perfect mental equilibrium. The same did not apply to councilor Galvan, whose accuracy in the objection made, and whose moderation in responding to the invectives of his colleagues, showed a well-organized brain on his part; for this reason, he asked the Council to deliver him. Feeling further aggrieved by councilor Galvan's conduct, the Council appreciated the alienist's request and unanimously voted for the delivery.

It is understood that, according to the new theory, a single fact or statement was not enough to admit someone to Green House; a long examination and a vast inquiry into the past and present were required. Father Lopes, for example, was only captured thirty days after the decree, and the apothecary's wife forty days. The confinement of this lady filled her spouse with indignation. Crispin Soares left home foaming with anger, declaring to anyone he encountered that he would tear the tyrant's ears off. An individual, an opponent of the alienist, hearing this news in the street, forgot the reasons for the dissent and rushed to Simon Bacamarte's house to inform him of the danger he faced. Simon Bacamarte showed gratitude for the opponent's behavior, and a few minutes were enough for him to recognize the rectitude of his feelings, human respect, and generosity; he shook his hands warmly and admitted him to Green House.

— A case like this is rare. — he said to the astonished woman. — Now let's wait for our Crispin.

Crispin Soares entered. Pain had overcome anger; the apothecary did not rip the ears off the alienist. The alienist consoled his private, assuring him that it was not a lost case; perhaps the woman had some brain injury; he would examine her very carefully, but before that, he couldn't leave her on the street. And, thinking it advantageous to reunite them, as the husband's cunning and roguery could somehow cure the moral beauty he had discovered in the wife, Simon Bacamarte said:

— You will work during the day at the apothecary shop, but you will have lunch and dinner with your wife, and you will spend the nights here, as well as Sundays and holidays.

The proposal put the poor apothecary in the situation of Buridan's donkey. He wanted to live with his wife but feared returning to Green House; and in this struggle, he stayed for some time until Mrs. Evarista took him out of the difficulty, promising to take care of the friend and convey messages between them. Crispin Soares kissed her hands gratefully. This last act of pusillanimous self-ishness seemed sublime to the alienist.

After five months, about eighteen people were lodged, but Simon Bacamarte did not slacken; he went from street to street, house to house, spying, questioning, studying; and when he found a sick person, he took them with the same joy with which he had gathered them by the dozens before. This disproportion itself confirmed the new the-ory; the true pathology of the brain had finally been found. One day, he managed to bring the judge from outside into Green House; but he proceeded with so much scrupulous-ness that he did so only after meticulously studying all his actions and questioning the town's leaders. More than once, he was on the verge of admitting perfectly unbal-anced people; this happened with a lawyer, whom he rec-ognized as possessing such a combination of moral and mental qualities that it was dangerous to leave him on the street. He had him arrested, but the agent, suspicious, asked him to conduct an experiment; he went to a friend, sued for a false will, and advised him to hire Sallustius as his lawyer; that was the name of the person in question.

— So, do you think…?

— Undoubtedly: go, confess everything, the whole truth, whatever it may be, and entrust the case to him.

The man went to the lawyer, confessed to having forged the will, and ended up asking him to take on the case. The lawyer did not refuse; he studied the papers, reasoned at length, and proved beyond a shadow of a doubt that the will was more than true. The defendant's innocence was solemnly proclaimed by the judge, and the inheritance passed into his hands. The distinguished jurist owed his freedom to this experience.

But nothing escapes an original and penetrating mind. Simon Bacamarte, who had been noticing for some time the zeal, sagacity, patience, and moderation of that agent, recognized the skill and tact with which he had carried out such a delicate and complicated experiment, and immediately decided to admit him to Green House; however, he gave him one of the best cubicles.

The insane were housed by classes. A gallery was made for the modest ones; that is, the madmen in whom this moral perfection predominated; another for the tolerant, another for the truthful, another for the simple, another for the loyal, another for the magnanimous, another for the sagacious, another for the sincere, etc. Naturally, the families and friends of the inmates protested against the theory, and some tried to compel the City Council to revoke the license. However, the Council had not forgotten the speech of councilor Galvan, and if they revoked the license, they would see him back on the street and restored to his position; therefore, they refused. Simon Bacamarte wrote to the councilors, not thanking them but congratulating them on this act of personal revenge.

Disillusioned with legality, some leading figures in the town secretly turned to the barber Porphyry and assured him of all the support of people, money, and influence at court if he led another movement against the City Council and the alienist. The barber replied that he would not; that ambition had led him the first time to break the laws, but he had corrected himself, recognizing his own mistake and the little consistency of the opinions of his followers; that the Council had authorized the alienist's new experiment for a year: it was necessary to either wait for the end of the term or appeal to the viceroy if the same Council rejected the request. He would never advise the use of a recourse that he saw fail in his hands and that too at the cost of deaths and injuries that would be his eternal remorse.

— What are you telling me? — asked the alienist when a secret agent told him about the barber's conversation with the town's leaders.

Two days later, the barber was admitted to Green House. — Caught for having a dog, caught for not having a dog! — Exclaimed the unfortunate man.

The end of the deadline arrived, and the City Council authorized an additional six-month period for testing therapeutic methods. The outcome of this episode from the Itaguai chronicle is of such a nature and so unexpected that it deserved no less than ten chapters of exposition; but I content myself with one, which will be the conclusion of the narrative and one of the finest examples of scientific conviction and human selflessness.

Chapter XIII: Plus Ultra!

It was time for therapy. Simon Bacamarte, active and sagacious in identifying the sick, exceeded himself in the diligence and insight with which he began to treat them. On this point, all the chroniclers are in full agreement: the illustrious alienist performs astonishing cures that aroused the liveliest admiration in Itaguai.

Indeed, it was challenging to imagine a more rational therapeutic system. With the mad divided into classes based on the moral perfection that exceeded in each of them, Simon Bacamarte took care to directly address the predominant quality. Suppose a modest person. He applied medication that could instill the opposite feeling, and he didn't immediately use maximum doses, — he graduated them according to the patient's condition, age, temperament, and social status. Sometimes, a coat, a ribbon, a wig, or a cane were enough to restore reason to the lunatic; in other cases, the illness was more stubborn; he then resorted to diamond rings, honorary distinctions, etc. There was a poet patient who resisted everything. Simon Bacamarte was beginning to despair of a cure when he had the idea to spread the news through town criers, proclaiming him as a rival to Garção and Pindar.

— It was a holy remedy, — the mother of the unfortunate man told a friend; — it was a holy remedy.

Another patient, also modest, opposed the same rebellion to the medication, but not being a writer (he could barely sign his name), the town crier remedy couldn't be applied to him. Simon Bacamarte thought of requesting for him the position of secretary of the Academy of the Concealed, established in Itaguai. The positions of president and secretaries were appointed by royal nomination, by the special grace of the late King Dom John V, and implied the treatment of Excellency and the use of a gold plate on the hat. The government of Lisbon rejected the diploma, but representing that he was not seeking it as an honorary reward or legitimate distinction but only as a therapeutic means for a difficult case, the government exceptionally yielded to the plea; and even then, not without extraordinary effort from the Minister of the Navy and Overseas, who happened to be a cousin of the lunatic. It was another holy remedy.

— Really, it's admirable! — people said in the streets, observing the healthy and puffed-up expressions of the two former lunatics.

Such was the system. The rest can be imagined. Each moral or mental beauty was attacked at the point where perfection seemed most solid, and the effect was certain. It was not always certain. There were cases where the predominant quality resisted everything; then the alienist attacked another part, applying to therapy the method of military strategy, which takes a fortress through one point if it cannot be achieved through another.

At the end of five and a half months, Green House was empty; everyone cured! Councilor Galvan, so cruelly afflicted with moderation and equity, had the fortune of losing an uncle; I say fortune because the uncle left an ambiguous will, and he obtained a favorable interpretation by corrupting the judges and confusing the other heirs. The sincerity of the alienist manifested itself in this incident; he candidly confessed that he had no part in the cure: it was the simple *vis medicatrix*[8] of nature. The same did not happen with Father Lopes. Knowing that he was completely ignorant of Hebrew and Greek, the alienist tasked him with making a critical analysis of the Septuagint version; the priest accepted the task, and he did it wisely; after two months, he had a book and freedom. As for the apothecary's wife, she did not stay in the cell assigned to her for long, and there, she did not lack affection.

— Why doesn't Crispin come to visit me? — she said every day.

They would answer her one thing or another; finally, they told her the whole truth. The worthy matron could not contain her indignation and shame. In her outbursts of anger, loose and vague expressions escaped her, such as:

— Scoundrel!… rogue!… ungrateful!… A scoundrel who has built houses at the expense of counterfeit and rotten ointments… Ah! Scoundrel!…

Simon Bacamarte noted that, even if the accusation contained in these words were not true, they were enough to show that the excellent lady was finally restored to perfect imbalance of faculties, and he promptly discharged her.

• • • • • • •

[8] "Healing force."

Now, if you imagine that the alienist was delighted to see the last guest leave Green House, you show that you still do not know our man. *Plus ultra*![9] That was his motto. It was not enough for him to have discovered the true theory of madness; he was not satisfied with having established the reign of reason in Itaguai. *Plus ultra*! He did not become happy; he became preoccupied, thoughtful; something told him that the new theory had, in itself, another and entirely new theory.

— Let's see, — he thought; — let's see if I finally arrive at the ultimate truth.

Library

He said this, walking along the vast hall where the richest library in His Majesty's overseas domains sparkled. A wide damask robe, fastened at the waist by a silk cord with gold tassels (a gift from a university), enveloped the

. . . .

[9] "Beyond."

majestic and austere body of the illustrious alienist. The wig covered an extensive and noble bald head acquired through daily scientific contemplations. The feet, not slender and feminine, not large and clumsy, but proportionate to the figure, were protected by a pair of shoes with buckles made of simple and modest brass. See the difference: — only luxury was noticeable in what originated from scientific sources; what specifically came from him bore the color of moderation and simplicity, virtues so fitting for a wise person.

This was how he went, the great alienist, from one end to the other of the vast library, immersed in himself, oblivious to all things except the obscure problem of cerebral pathology. Suddenly, he stopped. Standing by a window, with his left elbow resting on his open right hand, and his chin in his closed left hand, he asked himself:

— But were they really mad, and were they cured by me, — or what seemed like a cure was nothing more than the discovery of the perfect imbalance of the brain?

Digging deeper into this, here is the result he arrived at: the well-organized brains he had just cured were imbalanced like the others. Yes, he thought to himself, I cannot claim to have instilled in them a new feeling or faculty; both existed in a latent state, but they existed.

Having reached this conclusion, the illustrious alienist had two conflicting sensations, one of joy, the other of dejection. The joy was to see that, after long and patient investigations, constant work, and immense struggle with the people, he could assert this truth: — there were no mad people in Itaguai. Itaguai did not possess a single lunatic. But as soon as this idea refreshed his soul, another one appeared that neutralized the first effect; it was the idea of doubt. What! Would Itaguai not have a single well-adjusted brain? Would this absolute conclusion not be inherently erroneous and, therefore, not destroy the broad and majestic edifice of the new psychological doctrine?

The distress of the distinguished Simon Bacamarte is defined by Itaguai chroniclers as one of the most horrendous moral storms that have descended upon a man. But storms only strike the weak; the strong brace themselves against them and face the thunder. Twenty minutes later, the countenance of the alienist was illuminated by a gentle brightness.

— Yes, it must be that. — he thought.

That is it. Simon Bacamarte found in himself the characteristics of perfect mental and moral balance; it seemed to him that he possessed sagacity, patience, perseverance, tolerance, truthfulness, moral vigor, loyalty, all the qualities, in short, that could make up a perfect lunatic. He doubted immediately, to be sure, and even concluded that it was an illusion; but being a prudent man, he decided to convene a council of friends, whom he questioned frankly. The opinion was affirmative.

— No flaws?

— None. — said the assembly in unison.

— No vices?

— None.

— Everything perfect?

— Everything.

— No, impossible. — shouted the alienist. — I say I don't feel in myself that superiority that I have just seen defined so magnificently. It's sympathy that makes you speak. I examine myself and find nothing that justifies the excess of your kindness.

The assembly insisted; the alienist resisted; finally, Father Lopes explained everything with this concept worthy of an observer:

— Do you know why you don't see your elevated qualities, which we all admire? It's because you have another quality that enhances the others: — modesty.

It was decisive. Simon Bacamarte bowed his head simultaneously joyful and sad, and even more joyful than sad. Immediately, he withdrew to Green House. In vain, his wife and friends told him to stay, that he was perfectly sane and balanced: neither pleas nor suggestions nor tears detained him for a single moment.

— The issue is scientific, — he said; — it's a new doctrine, of which I am the first example. I embody both theory and practice.

— Simon! Simon! My love! — his wife said to him with tears streaming down her face.

But the illustrious doctor, with eyes ablaze with scientific conviction, closed his ears to his wife's longing and gently repelled her. Once the door of Green House was closed, he devoted himself to the study and cure of himself. Chroniclers say that he died seventeen months later in the same state he entered, without having achieved anything. Some go so far as to conjecture that there was never another madman in Itaguai besides him, but this opinion, based on a rumor that circulated since the alienist expired, has no other proof than the rumor itself; a dubious rumor, as it is attributed to Father Lopes, who had so fervently highlighted the qualities of the great man. Be that as it may, the burial was conducted with much pomp and rare solemnity.

The end.

www.ingramcontent.com/pod-product-compliance
Lightning Source LLC
Chambersburg PA
CBHW051441140726
47987CB00006B/2479